Grandma and Grandpa Bauer visited this Benedictine Monastary in Abbadiar Di Monte Olivetao Maggiore (Superior)

13-10 to 13-19 lived in caves + in 1320 started monastaries

Love to Eloise and Scarlett.

Grandma + Grandpa

August 24, 2019

THE MONASTERY CAT

The Monastery Cat

Written and Illustrated by

Sharon Wooding

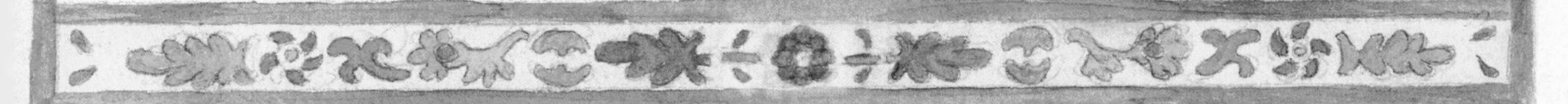

Printed in the United States of America on
FSC-certified, acid-free paper.

Designed by Mary A. Wirth
Author photo by Frances Lansing

ISBN 978-1-937650-79-7
Library of Congress Control Number: 2016953405

493 South Pleasant Street
Amherst, Massachusetts 01002
413.230.3943
smallbatchbooks.com

This book is dedicated to

Jerry Wooding, my husband, best friend, constant editor (no matter how busy or tired), and a champion of cats in monasteries and elsewhere, with much love and gratitude.

And for Frances Lansing, who introduced us to the Renaissance world and to the solitary wilderness of the Crete Senesi, and who in every way, for many years, has sustained Micio in his adventures.

Micio (mee'-cho):
the nickname given to all cats in Italy,
like "kitty" in America.

Through the downpour, as lightning lit up the sky, the cat could see a tall building at the top of the hill. At last he was out of the dark forest. He raced up the rocky slope and trotted to the open doorway.

A man in a white robe was sitting at a table.

Shaking his fur and twitching the raindrops off his whiskers, the cat padded over to the man and sat down.

The man looked up.

"Oh dear, poor Micio," he said. "Out on a night like this!" He sighed and petted the soggy cat.

"You look as wilted as I feel," he said. "I'm new here at the monastery, and I don't know the other monks very well. To tell the truth, I just want to go home."

Just then a big, important-looking monk stormed into the church.

"Brother Raffaele!" he grumbled. *"A cat in the monastery?!* You are not here to keep pets. You were sent to work on this project. And I see you have not gotten very far. The brothers are going to have a sublime lectern that will hold our great music book when you finish the piece . . . *if* you finish it!" And with that the big man shooed Micio back out into the rain, slammed the door, and left.

"That was the abbot," whispered Brother Raffaele letting the cat back in. "He's the head of the monastery, and he wants my lectern to make the abbey the talk of all of Italy . . . I'm trying.

"Come along, Micio. Tonight you can hide in my room. I'll show you the little pieces of wood that I'm putting in that lectern."

Micio followed Raffaele to the monk's room.

Before long, the weary cat was fast asleep by the fire.

The next morning, Micio awoke to the rattling of pots and got up to follow the aroma of food cooking.

"Micio," said Raffaele from the kitchen. "This is the Signora. She comes in sometimes to bake for the monks."

"Buon giorno," said the woman. "I heard about your terrible night—the storm, and how the abbot turned you out!"

Micio meowed and rubbed against Signora's leg in reply.

"The Signora is going to hide you in her pantry, Micio. The abbot never goes in there." The cat ventured over to see the little room as the Signora set down a bowl of bread and milk in the center of the kitchen.

Micio's tail quivered with delight when he saw it, but just as he was about to run over and tuck into his first meal in days . . .

. . . a mouse walked by the bowl! Then a second, then a third mouse!

The Signora grabbed a broom. "They'll eat everything in the abbey as well as the grain in the barn. Am I the only one here who notices these pests? There are more of them every day! There they go into the refectory!"

Micio bounded after the mice into the monks' dining room, and the mice, never having seen such a large animal in the monastery where they had just recently moved in, were terrified. They scurried under benches, and wove in and out between the legs of two monks who were clearing tables. Then all at once . . . CRASH . . . a tray of dishes clattered to the floor!

"WHAT? AGAIN!" shouted the abbot rushing in upon hearing the fracas. "Raffaele, why is that CAT still here?"

"W-well, Father Abbot," stammered Raffaele, "he was chasing the mice. You see, the monastery is getting . . ."

"The brothers here at the abbey," the abbot interrupted, "the most beautiful in all of Italy, tend daily to the wheat fields, the gardens, and the animals, and they make art in prayer books or, as you do, on lecterns. And their peace cannot be disturbed . . . by a CAT! Get rid of him!" And he turned on his heel, and stormed out the door.

"I can't let you go, Micio," said Raffaele. "Except for the Signora, you are my only friend here."

The Signora tiptoed in from the kitchen. "What if Micio were to stay in the barn?"

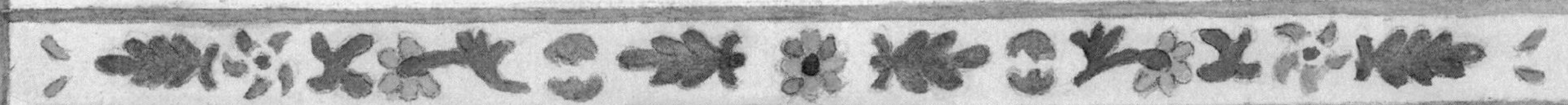

And so weeks went by as Micio made his home in a hayloft. The mice kept their distance from the cat, and the sacks of grain were now safe.

Micio would venture out at night back to the abbey, where he would quietly patrol the kitchen, the refectory, and even the abbot's rooms. He would stroll through the cloister where, in the moonlight, he could now see pictures on the walls. And he would visit the church where Raffaele was making the designs on his lectern more and more beautiful. The mice hid, never knowing when the big cat was going to appear, and finally some began to leave the monastery!

One morning, just as the sun rose, when Micio was leaving the abbey, he heard a new voice in the cloister.

"Grazie, Father Abbot. I'm glad you approve." Micio crept around a corner and saw a man holding a paintbrush, and a helper stirring something in a pail.

"Magnifico!" exclaimed the abbot to the painter. "We will be famous with your fantastic fresco glorifying our cloister walls, as we will be with the new lectern in the church!"

Micio looked up and saw what the painter and the abbot were too busy to notice . . . mice . . . an army of them . . . on the painter's work table . . . gobbling up his breakfast!

The cat forgot himself, jumped up onto the table, and as the mice scattered, he pounced, knocking over the artist's brushes and sending paint pots flying.

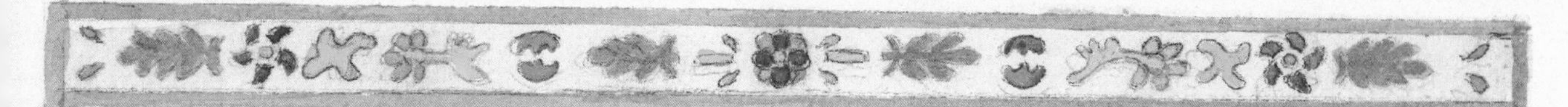

"NO!" shouted the painter's helper.

"My precious colors!" cried the artist.

"RAF . . . RAF . . . RAFFAELE!" shouted the abbot.

The horrified young monk came running down the hall in his nightclothes. The abbot was ready to explode. As Micio turned to get away, his tail brushed a candle flame and caught fire. The cat tore out of the cloister.

"I hope you're happy, Brother Raffaele! Look at this mess! Thank goodness, your cat is gone once and for all!"

Micio zigzagged through the forest and ran and ran until he spotted a pond. Normally, he hated getting wet. But now, with his tail on fire, he had no choice! Micio plunged into the blessedly cool water, which swallowed up the fire.

Luckily, the abbot had not followed him and, luckier still, Micio spied a fish, and finally enjoyed a meal fit for a cat. He found a cave and settled in, sneaking back each night to the fishpond for his tasty dinners. But he was not happy. His days at the abbey with his friend had truly come to an end.

One day Micio heard humming near his cave. It was Raffaele, picking berries. The cat was overcome with joy, and scrambled up on his friend's shoulder.

"Micio," cried the monk. "You must come back with me, back to the church. Oh . . ."

But Micio's ears drew back in fear.

"No, it's all right now. The abbot knows that the mice were fleeing the monastery all during the weeks when you were there. But they've come back. They're eating the crops. They're underfoot in the church and scampering everywhere. No one can work. The mice are driving the monks to distraction! And the abbey may have to close."

Micio slowly followed Raffaele back to the church.

The brothers stood, singing, around Raffaele's lectern, which was now finished.

"Look here, Micio," said the abbot reaching down to pet the nervous cat. "Raffaele has put someone very important to the monastery on our lectern."

Micio blinked at the sight that met his eyes. He saw a stately striped cat made out of tiny pieces of different colored wood: brown, gold, orange . . . that cat was Micio!

"We need you here," said the abbot. "Please stay."

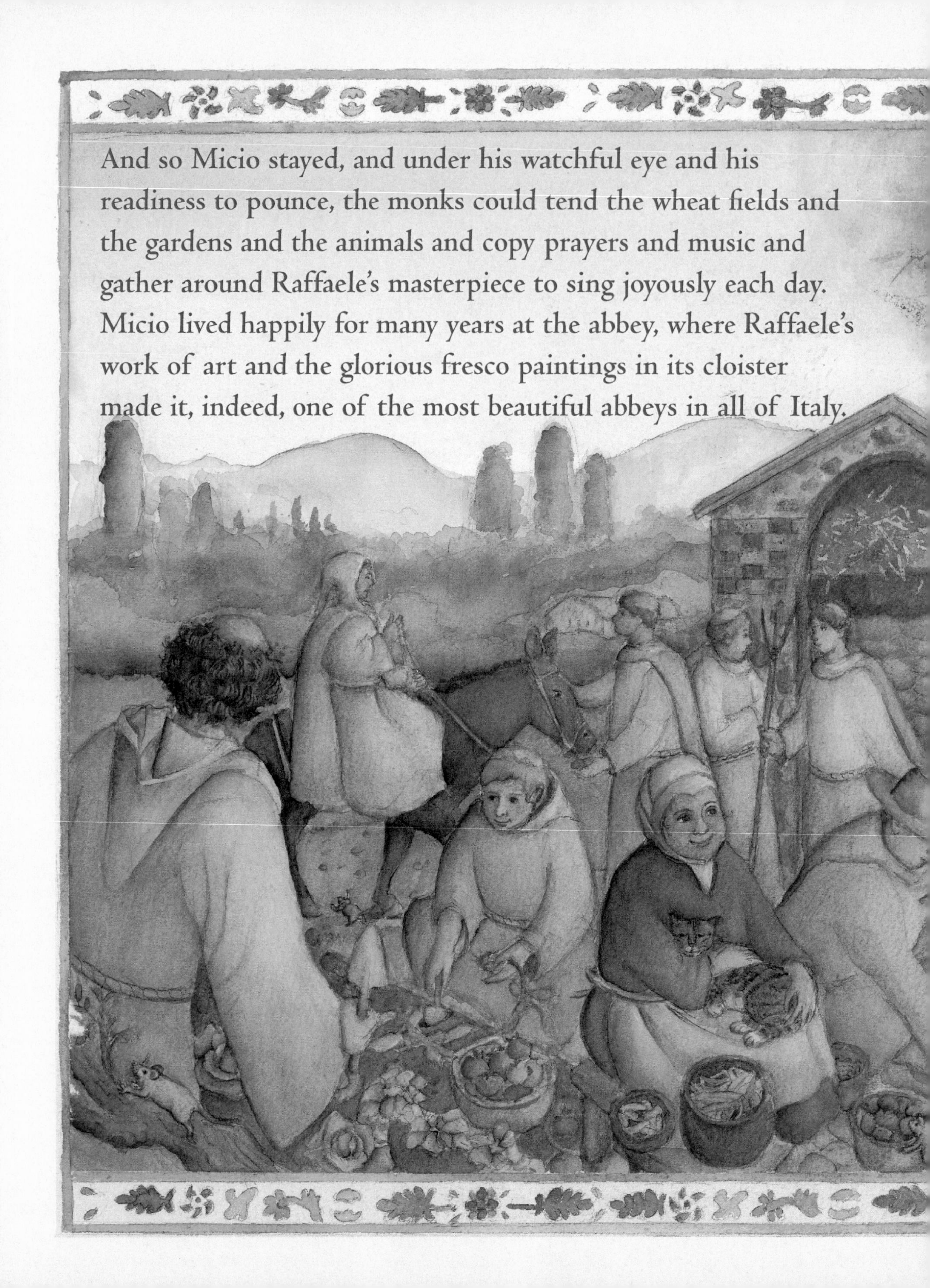

And so Micio stayed, and under his watchful eye and his readiness to pounce, the monks could tend the wheat fields and the gardens and the animals and copy prayers and music and gather around Raffaele's masterpiece to sing joyously each day. Micio lived happily for many years at the abbey, where Raffaele's work of art and the glorious fresco paintings in its cloister made it, indeed, one of the most beautiful abbeys in all of Italy.

Even the mice were content. They took to scurrying and playing around Micio, daring one another to get close to him, but knowing the whole time who was really in charge—
Micio, the monastery cat.

— FINIS —

BONONIE · FABREFACTVM

AUTHOR'S NOTE

Monasteries are private places where monks live together—praying, often in song, and working at their various jobs to help in the running of their home. This story takes place in a particularly beautiful monastery called Abbazia di Monte Oliveto Maggiore, which is hidden among olive trees in the rugged hills of a part of Italy called Tuscany. Monte Oliveto is known for its exquisite frescoes, or wall paintings, that tell the story of the life of Saint Benedict. Long ago, an artist from Siena named Giovanni Antonio Bazzi painted the scenes on the cloister walls. He painted the story in wet plaster, which is why the pictures are still bright and beautiful after 500 years.

Monte Oliveto Maggiore is also known for its big wooden lectern, or bookstand, which was carved at about the same time and which can still be seen in the monastery. In the 1500s, when printing presses were new and books were rare, monks would gather around a lectern and sing as their director read the music from a huge book. The songs had been copied and illustrated by hand by monks, bound into books, and placed on the big stand. Fra Raffaele da Brescia, or Brother Raffaele from Brescia, was the monk who inserted at the bottom of the lectern a picture of a cat made of hundreds of pieces of wood from different kinds of trees. No one knows why Raffaele put a tabby cat in his lectern, but in this make-believe story, Raffaele shows great respect for a creature who kept the monastery free from mice. That cat could very well have been Micio.

Indeed, descendants of the cat roam Monte Oliveto to this day.

ABOUT THE AUTHOR

Born and raised on Staten Island, New York, Sharon Wooding received her B.S. from Bucknell University and studied drawing and painting at the University of Colorado, the DeCordova Museum School, and the School of the Museum of Fine Arts, Boston. The illustrator of many books for children, including her own *Arthur's Christmas Wish* (Atheneum) and *The Painter's Cat* (Putnam), Wooding got the idea for *The Monastery Cat* during frequent visits to the Benedictine monastery of Monte Oliveto Maggiore, in Tuscany.

Wooding is a signature member of the New England Watercolor Society, where she served on the board for many years. She lives in a 200-year-old farmhouse in Groton, Massachusetts, with her husband, Jerry; their dog, Isabelle; and cat, Widget. To find out more about Sharon Wooding, visit sharonwooding.com

ACKNOWLEDGMENTS

I would like to express my appreciation to my dear family and friends for their encouragement, advice, and patience during the creation of *The Monastery Cat*. Many thanks to Claudia and Caleb Bach, who joyously followed the project from its inception to the last spot illustration, and to Suzanne Lavin, who jumped in and helped me, finally, to make the story work. Also thanks to Anson Wooding and Jack and Michael Templeton and the rest of the amazing monk models, and to Trisha Thompson and Fred Levine at Small Batch Books, who gave *The Monastery Cat* such loving care.

Lightning Source UK Ltd.
Milton Keynes UK
UKRC02n0455111018
330222UK00004B/11